Hard to Be Six

BY ARNOLD ADOFF
ILLUSTRATED BY CHERYL HANNA

Lothrop, Lee & Shepard Books   **New York**

First Edition   1 2 3 4 5 6 7 8 9 10

Library of Congress Cataloging in Publication Data
Adoff, Arnold. Hard to be six / Arnold Adoff ; illustrated by Cheryl Hanna.
p.   cm. Summary: A six-year-old boy who wants to grow up fast learns a lesson
about patience from his grandmother. ISBN 0-688-09013-3.
—ISBN 0-688-09579-8 (lib. bdg.) [1. Growth—Fiction.] I. Hanna, Cheryl, ill.
II. Title. PZ.A2616Har 1991 [E]—dc20
89-45903 CIP AC

For Jaime Levi   Finally and Always

A.A.

For Dad—the lines, the form, and the shadows
For Mom—the colors and the light

C.H.

This sunshine Sunday afternoon,
we have a party behind our house
for my big sister: ten today.
    There is chocolate cake and
ice cream. Big girls singing: happy.
    My birthday sister shuts her
eyes and wishes. She blows all the
candles out. We sing and shout on
a backyard afternoon: big girls,
tall cousins, and one small
brother wishing: soon.
    This little brother is still
six. I will try to eat more cake
and read the words right off the
ice-cream box. I run my fastest in
the games, and still end: last.

Hard to be six.

Hard to be six
when your sister is ten.
There are things she can do that
must wait until then: when I am
seven or eight, nine or ten.
Hard to be six until then.
I always pin the tail on the
donkey's foot, or on his anklebone,
or on his knee. Me. I never hit his
back. I never reach his rear.

But in a muddy corner of our yard,
I can mix a made-up mud mix, and build
a highway for my fire truck to come and
save the people. In the mud, the big red
truck has gone too fast around a curve
and crashed, and smashed my mixer
mixing mix. I can fix.

Later on I have to go to bed: before.
And I can't eat my popcorn from the bowl,
or drink my milk right on the floor,
like she can do. I still spill.

Under the covers, I pretend I am the
brave fire chief, climbing up the ladder
to save the people. But my big yellow
boots are stuck, and I have to move fast.
I have to reach taller to the top.

I wake up in a hurry to be big.

Monday is a bad day: no one
comes to play with me. But big
sister has her friends out around
the block. They kick my soccer ball,
and take turns on my bike.

Then I take Sis's brand-new
bike, and ride it only in our yard.
I crash it in the old and ivy fence.
Sister screams and Momma runs to see.

The big girls laugh and talk
that baby brother talk: "You know
how they are, those little kids."

I feel so small and sorry
that I fell and banged the bike,
and banged my knee. Me and knee.

Hard to be six
when your sister is ten:
when you want to be big right away,
and stay with that big bike
around the house until dark.

Eight o'clock when I kiss Sis
good night. (We always kiss good
night.) She asks me:
"How's the knee?" (It still feels
sore.) She tells me not to worry.
"The bike and both of us
are OK to the end."

Sis says to think about all
the good things: about growing each
night long; about growing tall, right
past the last mark on the bedroom wall.
"Think about the best things you can do:
shirt into pants, shoelaces into shoe."

In bed before I fall asleep,
I pretend I am the biggest
ten-year-old on the biggest
ten-speed bike. I am flying
out of our yard and down the street.
I reach pedals. I reach brakes.
I work that big bike fast and best.

Now time to rest.

Tuesday is a rain in afternoon day: cold and gray. Momma plays with me and my trains. We build long tunnels out of blocks, and pretend that rocks slide down the mountain onto the tracks.

We pull the people from the wreck and save them all.

When the trains are back on track we sit and watch them run. Momma talks about the fun we have together, and about how big I am growing: "Feet are too big for your shoes again.

"New shoes before old ones are worn out and full of holes, is the best news I know to tell," she says. "And sneakers too, before this month is hardly through."

Then Daddy brings the dinner out,
and calls:
"It is time, it is time."
We are all hungry for good food
and laughing.
My burger is big as any.
My belly is full as all.
Daddy still says he uses his secret
seasoning each time, to grow me tall.

In my good bed, inside the circle
of the tracks, I pretend I am the engineer
driving the train. I pull the rope that
sounds the whistle, as the train rolls
faster around the mountain slope.

I wave my big hand
to all the little boys.

And just before I fall asleep,
the shoe-store man is shouting:
"Stop! Please clear the track and
sit right down, while I bring more
boxes from the back. I know I have
your very big, big size."

Sleep.
No creep to kitchen sink
for sixteen drinks of water.

No peep. Deep sleep to help
me grow my ten long toes.

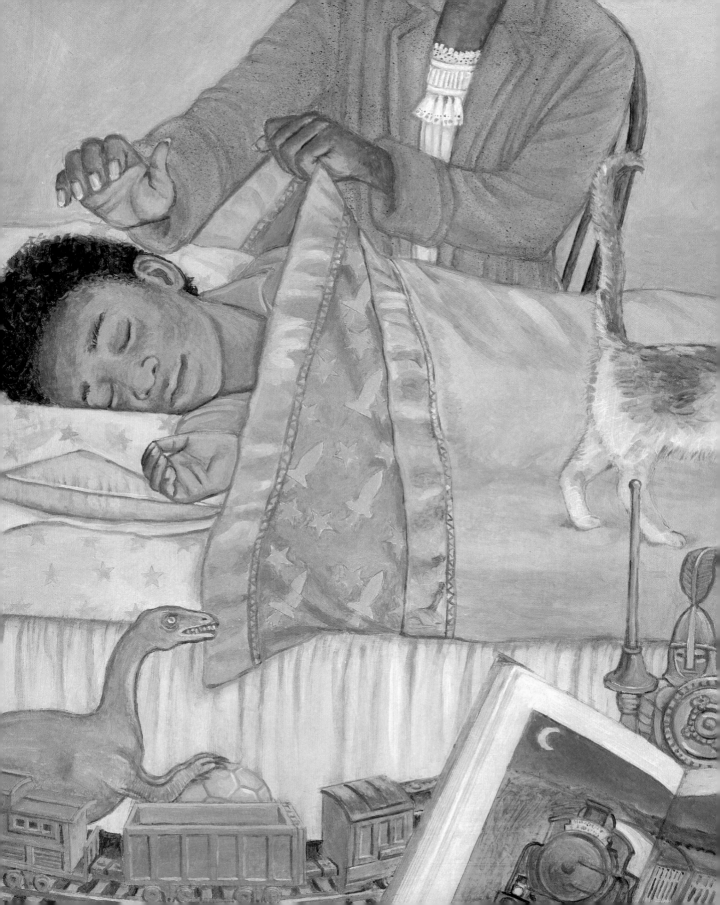

Next morning we eat real fast.
Dad says: "Hurry with those chores.
We have someplace special to go."

We get on the bus. Just us in back:
our feet up on the hump over the wheels.
The bouncing ride feels good, through
our city streets and over to the park.
  I watch the people step down
to the door, and step outside. Away.
Outside, the trees are up to the sun,
and the little dogs are just down low.

  Daddy says, "Everything grows
from the ground up, from younger
and small, to older and tall. All."
I think we must be growing, as we
go on this bus. All of us: together.
  I know the world is round,
  is going round:
  all of us on the same ride.

Here in our park, this Wednesday
carousel has splashing, dashing horses.
When the music stops, the ticket-taking
man must come to take my belt off and
help me down.
Goodbye horses. Goodbye clown.

All the way home on the bus again,
we talk about waiting for the big things.
I know I will write and read, skate
and speed around the block before
too long. Big and strong.
Growing up must be like this
big old bus back home: It always
gets there in the end. But slow. Slow.

In bed at night, I'm not the one
who holds on tight. I pretend to make
the ticket-taking man wear that belt.
I help him down. "Be careful, little
guy," I say, and send him on his way.

I wake up making plans to play.

Hard to be six
in this Sunday morning car
to Grandma's house: a far ride
on a hot day. I am strapped in
under seatbelts all the way.
I can't see out the window, or
up ahead. Slow ride: inside.

Grandma has: candy in little
dishes on all the tables, and after-
dinner ice cream with green cherries.
Every cookie you could think is good
to eat is in the jars on the counter
by the kitchen sink.
And the nicest about Grandma
is always the walk around her house
and over to the walnut tree.
Quiet as two mice in sneakers we walk.
Quiet as two mice we talk. The nicest
about Grandma is always listening to me.

Then Grandma says:
"Hard to be any age, so true.
Just hard to be six or ten or thirty-
three, or seventy. Seventy especially.

"Older people always say to younger
ones: 'Just wait, and drink your milk.
You'll grow in time.' We all want to hold
on to the passing past, to make the
present moments last.

"Now help me get these stiff
old bones back to home. I need
some rest. Then later on this
afternoon we'll take a ride.
I want to show you something
that will help inside.
"You know I love you,
and I love your pride. You're
big enough right now to help
me walk and listen to my talk.
Your grandpa would have loved
to squeeze that muscle
in your arm."

When the car stops, we let Grandma
go on ahead. She wants to put some flowers
down, and be alone. It looks like she is
talking. Then Grandma calls for us
to come and see his name:
"Grandpa you never knew.

"He would have loved to know you both.

"He would have loved you both.

"This stone for Grandpa shows it all.
Here is when he was born. He lived a good
long time. And here is when he died:
numbers, years."

Grandma says he always tried his best:
no tears.

Here are words I can read alone:
out loud.

Take   Time   Slow
Make   Life   Count
Pass   Love   On

Then Grandma smiles
and hugs us both,
and hugs us proud.

All the way back home, in our car,
my eyes are mostly closed. But one time
I wake against Daddy's shoulder. Momma
and Sis are talking in the front:
becoming that, becoming this.
　　And the sky is black
　　and full of stars.

　　In bed at night, home and warm
and covered tight, I pretend I am
hopping around that sky, counting
stars as I flash by. My yellow
boots have jets that shoot red fire
streams. I fly through my almost
dreams and say hello to Grandpa.

"Grandpa: I will learn to ride
that bike, and cursive write, and tie
those laces tight.
And try to learn to wait.
    "From me to you, I'll take time slow,
and make life count, and pass love on,
                          and on and on.
    "From you to me.
From me to you.
From here to far away."

In the morning I wake up slow
and sleepy. Ready for the day.

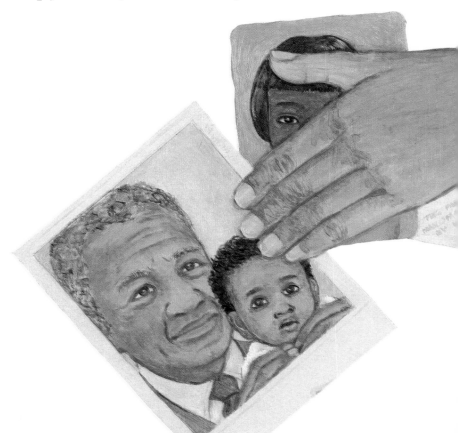